Found In Misty Falls: A Story of Magic

A Cursed Antique, Volume 2

Martha Wickham

Published by Martha Wickham, 2015.

FOUND IN MISTY FALLS: A STORY OF MAGIC

First edition. February 7, 2015.

ISBN: 979-8224842551

Written by Martha Wickham.

Chapter 1:
Finding The Ring

Violet was hiking near the mountains, when she saw it. She had stopped to catch her breath and take in the scenery when something shiny caught her eye. Something was sparkling in the sun like metal, slightly hidden under the brush. Before she could lose sight of it, she decided to investigate.

Her brown braids flew in the air as she ran to it. It was a ring. It had six large diamonds on it, set in some shiny silver. The ring was polished and not the type of shiny that you see in your daily life. It commanded attention, almost as if it was calling to Violet, and the more she looked at it, the more difficult it got for her to resist the temptation to pick up the object.

Shrouded in confusion, Violet was not sure if the ring was real. However, she was still drawn to it. She still found it pretty.

Who would be stupid enough to lose a ring like that on a mountain trail? Or even wear a ring like that on a hike, if it were real.

After reasoning with herself, Violet gave in and put it on, pushing it out of her mind. She continued with the trek.

Violet was used to these hikes; her parents would bring her here as a kid and spend their time together. It was all about peace and tranquility that this place brought her – she would enjoy her time here on the trails as it would allow her to clear her mind. Not to forget, she had fallen in love with the scenery. The workout was good too. It let her relax and think. And she liked getting away from the house sometimes to give herself a break from schoolwork and the hassle of everyday chores.

She came on these hikes whenever possible, but sometimes they just became exhausting. She would venture farther than she knew, entranced with nature, and then realize how far she had come. The same happened this time; she reached the trail's end, broke out of her reverie, and got carried away basking into the nature around her.

It had been a long time since Violet had the chance to feel the way she wanted. However, her mum would be mad at her for coming home late.

Violet looked at her watch; it said it was five forty in the evening. It would take her another hour to get back home at least, and the worst of all, the sun was going down, and it was getting dark.

The silver lining here was that Violet had a headlamp with her, something that her dad had advised her to bring, especially in cases such as this one.

She found herself regretting her decision to come out and decided to stop for a bit. She was ruing the long trek back. She was concerned about the outcome and how her parents would react, especially her mother, as Violet did not want her mother to be mad at her for being so late.

"I wish I were at home," she said, and then all of a sudden, there was a darkness that engulfed Violet. It was as if the sun had died all of a sudden.

Violet opened her eyes to bright light. Raising her hands to shield her eyes from the light, she bent back, thinking it was a UFO or something. Her heart dropped when she realized what it was. Violet did not see a UFO or grey people who were out to kidnap her. No, the light was the flood light her dad had installed outside her house. Violet was home.

Okay. What?

Violet was baffled as to what had happened. Thinking she had blacked out or something on the way home, she checked her watch. It was five forty in the evening. Same date. Same time. Not a minute had passed. It took Violet some time to wrap her head around what had happened – you do not get to witness such events every day, and sometimes, not in your entire life.

"Oh-kay. What?" Violet raised her right hand to her left arm, giving it a pinch. It hurt. "Alright. Guess I'm not dreaming then," Violet confirmed to herself.

While lowering her hand, her eyes caught sight of the ring. It was glowing now. After putting it on, she had not even thought about it, and now she found that this beautiful ring was warm and glowing. It was looking real now. Real weird. Violet began to think that the magic trick and the ring were connected.

At that point, she knew the ring was magic. That made her want to tell her mother. Whom else was she going to tell? However, this posed another question for Violet. How was she going to break it to her mother about what she had just witnessed?

Violet was under the impression that the ring was magical, but we lived in a world where magic did not occur out of nowhere. For all Violet knew, the ring could have been something malicious, and she could have been in danger.

Thoughts ran into Violet's head as she tried to figure out what needed to be done and how to proceed forward with the situation at hand. Was she going to tell her parents? Was she going to keep the ring? What if she decided to get rid of the ring altogether? There were countless possibilities surrounding just the ring and what needed to be done with it. Indeed, it confused Violet.

After contemplating what needed to be done with the ring, Violet decided to break the news to her parents — hoping they would understand the situation and provide more helpful insight into the case. After all, she was just a 15-year-old girl; in her mind, this was just an adventure.

Her parents, the adults, knew the world and all that inhabited it much better. They were the only people who would be able to offer not just a sound opinion but would also shield Violet from anything malicious that could be after her.

After talking to herself, Violet decided what needed to be done and how this situation would be handled. She mustered the courage and decided to walk into her home, confident that whatever happened, her parents would not abandon her or scold her for doing something hastily.

Chapter 2:
Where Did It Come From?

Violet walked into the house and ensured that she was not behaving outlandishly; she wanted to make sure that she was her usual self and that this situation was not getting out of hand. One must be composed in the face of conflict; if this ring had any dispute, Violet and her parents would handle it like adults.

Later that night, she asked her parents to help determine where it came from. It was a debate for her. However, at that time, Violet did not tell them about this ring's supposed magic. It was still a thing of wonder for her, but at the same time, she wanted to be sure that the ring was safe for her to be around.

Violet finally gathered the courage to tell her parents about the ring and the magic it had in it. It was not easy; after all, a 15-year-old telling their parents that they had just witnessed magic is not something that happened every day.

Violet, however, managed to do just that. It was an odd conversation, but her parents took the magic side as a kid's flight of fancy. Violet did not want to correct them. In her mind, finding out where the ring came from would be enough.

After all, if Violet had just dumped everything onto her parents or tried convincing them otherwise, things could have gotten out of hand, and Violet did not want that, and she was certain that her parents did not want that either.

"We can put an ad in the paper and see if anyone claims it," her dad proposed.

Violet realized that things were not getting out of hand, and her dad, being a father, was being as sensible as one could be to a startled teenager. To Violet, it seemed like the best idea at the time, and so they decided to do that.

In the meantime, it was decided that the ring would stay on Violet's finger. Her parents had not considered the consequences of leaving a magic ring in possession of a teenager, but since they had not thought it could be magic, they let it be. It might strike one as weird, but they trusted Violet and knew that all these years of experience would not have allowed things to get out of hand for them or Violet.

Her parents were helpful by posting an ad in the local papers' lost and found section the next day. They took a picture of Violet's hand with the ring on it so people would recognize it. For them and Violet, this was the best thing one could do since trying to find the owner by going door to door was not something that would have been possible.

However, Violet's father knew about the ring. He did not realize it on his account but heard about it from someone else after they called him, enquiring about the ring.

He just decided not to tell Violet about the story as it would have complicated things further for her, and that was not what he wanted as a father.

Close to her sixteenth birthday, her dad told her someone had a story about the ring. Someone had called and told him about the ring and where it came from. Once Violet's father broke the story to her, it all started making sense. He, being gentle he was, asked Violet to sit down and listen to the story. He started the conversation by telling Violet that she could keep the ring. Of course, Violet was happy to hear it. She wasn't only used to having the ring on her finger, but it had powers, which Violet had not had the experience with before. It was something that she was excited about and how it would turn out.

However, before the conversation ended, Violet's father decided that his daughter needed to know more about where the ring came from and what power it held.

***

Violet's father continued with the story and told her that the ring once belonged to a girl about twenty-five years ago. She was in a circus that passed through here. She wore it in the woods one day; however, little did the girl know that there was a magician meddling with the occult, and she just happened to be there as the magician was trying to meddle with forces that were beyond his understanding.

After all, magic is not something that humans know everything about. This meant things did not always go as planned whenever someone tried to meddle with magic. That was precisely what happened to the magician as well.

While the girl was in the forest, something happened there that caused all this. The magician tried to take the essence of his magic and put it in the ring. At that time, no one knew if it was a blessing or the ring was cursed, but something happened before she could figure out what it was.

It jumped off her finger, and they never figured out where it went. They even tried looking for it, but the ring was lost, and they even thought it was for good.

Her father knew this story because it spread across town after the girl returned from the woods and told everyone. One does not hold back such information, at least not in those times when everything was up for public amusement.

However, it did not stop there, as the magician did not give up his quest and approach the girl after the ring incident. When the magician approached the girl, she was not delighted to see him. She got mad and said, "That wasn't funny. That wasn't yours."

"Sorry, my name is Brian. I'm good at magic, but I still like to practice. I'm a magician."

"I'm Cara." She began going around searching for her ring. She still wanted that ring; it must have meant something to her.

However, Brian seemed unfazed by the fact that Cara had lost her ring and was also trying to find it.

"I can get you a new one."

"Okay. I have to perform in the circus the next few nights. Wearing a green sequined outfit and walking a tightrope."

"Great, I'll come. We'll have dinner and make it a date."

"That would be good. Do you mean a romantic date?"

"Just as friends. Unless you want it to be a romantic date?"

Cara acted relieved but noticing how attractive he was made her feel bad. Maybe she was disappointed that he did not say it would be a romantic date. She was interested in knowing what a magician like him could do.

She was eager for the date, romantic or otherwise. She wanted to know more about Brian and his magic. It was not every day you stumble upon a magician, at least not someone good or handsome like Brian.

"This is neat. A magical ring!"

"I enchanted it with a special enchantment. I meant for it to be powerful. You can use it almost like a magic wand.

You know, like the one in the stories."

She looked for the ring calling out to it, "Ring!"

It heard her and wanted to go to her, but it couldn't because it didn't know exactly where she had gone. It sparkled as she wandered farther away with her new friend.

"I'll get you a free ticket to the circus tonight," she said, smiling.

"Okay, that would be great." They smiled at each other and returned to the circus tent where she stayed nearby.

With the whole situation clear and the story finally unveiling itself, Violet could not help but wonder if it was some game fate pulled that the ring made its way to her. But she was excited to have it nonetheless. Now that her father has said that she could keep it, things would only get better for her, and there were limitless possibilities.

Violet started thinking about endless things that she would do with the ring and also started imagining all the magic that was inside the ring. Who would not be excited to have something so powerful and enchanted in their hands? It could be used to achieve a million things without ever having to work for them.

However, having the ring aside, Violet was still confused and scared. She had some idea about what the ring could do, but she did not know what else was there that could take place. If something can be used for good, it can also be used for something terrible.

The excitement in Violet's head was coupled with confusion and fear, but since she was with her father at that moment, there was a sense of safety and assurance that whatever happens, her father, at least, would not let the situation get out of hand.

When Violet's dad stopped talking, her mother, Deborah, came out and sat on the couch.

Violet didn't know if she wanted a magic ring. She still could not figure out whether having the ring was good or bad.

What did the enchantment do? She lifted her hand and pointed it at a potted plant.

"Alakazam!"

WHACK

The whole plant whipped back as if a gust of wind hit it.

It was magic!

"Maybe we should find the owner and return it."

Violet's cloudy judgment had almost convinced her that she wanted to find the owner and give the ring back, and at the same time, she was very insistent on keeping the ring to her. In her mind, the ring could threaten her family and herself, and at the same time, she was enchanted by a million things that could be achieved just by having the ring and the magic it possessed.

Before she could act on her benevolent idea of finding and returning the ring to its rightful owner, something in Violet's mind lit up, and she had another thought that changed her mind.

Violet had no idea about the ring or what endless things it could do. So, how about she tried to learn more about the ring?

Maybe she could find a book about magic and some actual magic words to use. Violet was thinking about all the ways the ring could be used and all the magic it had in it. And then ... something happened with the ring.

The magic in it made the diamond give off a bright white twinkle. This fascinated Violet and the ring's thoughts took over her again.

All the attention she had put towards the story her father was telling her was now directed towards what the ring had done in front of her.

Her dad looked at her like he wanted to continue the story. Quickly she turned straight ahead and listened. She did not want her dad to think she was not listening to him.

She was prone to flights of fancy and spacing out at times, and she did not want her dad to know she had spaced out again, especially when he wanted to tell a story. For all she knew, the story could have been crucial in helping her understand that the ring did much more than she knew.

As a teenager, she knew not to mess with her parents. She wanted her dad to know how well she listened next time the questions of sleepover permissions or grounding rules were nigh.

How far would this magic go? she wondered. Would it work at school and help her on a test? She believed it would go very far.

In her heart, Violet was aware of the fact that she knew very little about the ring, so she spent the rest of the night trying to come up with all the ways that the ring would work and how it would help her make things better and different at school, in her life and more. Before she could return to the dreaming world again, her father started the story again.

***

Everything went smoothly that night as the circus went on. Walking across the tightrope, Cara could see Brian out there. She made eye contact with him in the crowd multiple times that performance, despite her stunts requiring her full attention.

It was as if Cara was enchanted by Brian and wanted to know what this seemingly new chapter in her life held for her.

At the show's end, he came to her tent with flowers.

"You ready to go to dinner?"

She had a new dress on and replied, "Yeah."

They went to a nearby restaurant and had a nice spaghetti dinner. The Bolognese sauce was spectacular, though the pasta itself was not as cooked as it could have been.

The dinner could have been a lot better, but thanks to Brian's charm and company, Cara's evening went just fine, and she enjoyed it a lot more than she would have had she been alone.

Brian went ahead and placed a box on the table and said, "This is your replacement ring."

She opened it up and was mesmerized by it. The ring that Brian gave to Cara was unlike the ring she had lost back in the woods – it looked more refined and more expensive. But Cara was not going to turn it down. The ring Brian gave Cara had three diamonds, a larger diamond complemented by two smaller ones. Cara decided to put it on.

"This one is not enchanted. It's just enchanting, isn't it?

"Unless you want it to be so in more ways than one, I can make this a magic ring if you want me to."

"No thanks." She admired it as she walked home with him.

It was the start of a beautiful relationship. When the two arrived at her door, she asked,

"How did you like the show?"

"It was great. I had fun watching you."

"Good," she said sweetly and kissed him on the cheek.

Violet's father continued with the story about the night when Cara and Brian met for the first time.

After that date at the restaurant, Brian never missed a chance to show up at the circus and see Cara. Both started dating soon, and all the happiness surrounding Cara made her forget about the old ring.

Cara and Brian shared a bond that was not going to end just like that; that is why when the circus ended, and she had to leave, Brian followed her wherever she went.

They were together a long time and managed to still be together through thick and thin. That is why when Brian proposed to her, Cara did not think twice and said yes to him, He gave her an engagement ring, and she said, "This reminds me of the ring you gave me after you made me lose the first one." They giggled at the memory.

They were both happy, happy, and in love. Careless about what the future holds. Sure, they were looking forward to their life together, but at that moment, they had unwavering love and support for each other.

***

"That ring you found has been out there ever since," Violet's father said.

"Well, I'm going to keep it for a while and see what it can do. What could be neater than having a magical ring, dad?" She was excited, kissed her mom on the cheek, and then went to her room. She could not wait for school the next day, and the possibilities of what the ring could do made the prospect of school even more exciting.

Violet was like any other teenager, filled to the brim with all the dreams and possibilities that waited for her in the world. To make it all better, she had a magic ring, which would only be the start of her time with this ring.

Who knew what the future is going to be like? For Violet, this was just the beginning of something magical that could change so much for her in life at the age of just 15.

Violet had felt like the luckiest teenager, much better than anyone she had known for a long time. She was sitting in her chair; her mother called her to the phone. There was a call for Violet; she got excited and couldn't wait to tell everyone about the magic ring.

It was her friend on the phone; Violet excitedly told her friend everything.

"Is that all you care about?" Tammy asked in a cold, snotty voice.

Defensively she replied, "No, no, it's not. I have my health and was also considering getting a pet."

"I wish for a black cat," she whispered away from the receiver.

Suddenly a black cat came running around the corner to her, appearing out of thin air. Violet was surprised at first but then realized she possessed a magic ring. She then petted the cat and said, "I'll name you Darkness."

That evening she came to the dinner table with the cat, surprising her parents, and asked if she could keep the cat.

"Yes, as long as you care for him, keep your room clean, and do your homework."

"Deal," Violet said to her mother as she began eating macaroni and cheese; she was ecstatic that she was getting the chance to keep Darkness. Especially knowing the fact that this cat was perhaps born out of magic, and this would have easily scared other people away.

Violet quickly started thinking about how much fun it would be to keep the ring with her and all the things she could do with it.

Chapter 3:
Bring Your Ring To School Day

It was finally time to head to the school, and as expected, Violet was very excited. She had her ring on as expected, and the excitement could also be seen on her face. Her friend approached her near the lockers, "Hi Vi."

"Hi," she answered.

"What are you up to?"

"I'm going to class."

She saw that Violet's ring was shimmering. It quickly grabbed her attention, just like it got Violet's attention the first time she saw the ring.

"What's that?" she asked.

"You're not going to believe this, but I found something magical. This ring was on the ground when I was hiking. My dad wanted to see the owner, but I got to keep it.

We found out where this ring came from, though. My dad told me the whole story when someone reached out about it. A magician put an enchantment into it."

Violet checked her folder. "It will be lunch after this next class."

She realized she had no money on her for lunch. However, Violet tried her best to remain calm and composed. She continued, "My lunch money is gone. It was four dollars to buy something for lunch. The owners left town with the circus. Do you want to go to a circus with me sometime?"

"Sure," she answered. "I've got to go through. I have class. I'll see you at lunch."

Violet went to her classroom and wondered what had happened to her money. As class started and the teacher talked, she noticed some students snickering behind her. She turned around. One of them looked at her funny. It occurred to her then that they were the culprits stealing her money.

She left her folder unattended sometimes. They must have taken it after she walked away. She knew that they weren't very friendly, to begin with. So, she decided to seek help from the ring, and as expected, the ring was delivered. "Ring, please help me," she whispered.

When class was over, everyone went outside. Violet approached the ringleader of the group. She assumed he was the one that had her money.

"I believe you took my lunch money. Let me have it back."

"You can smell it on me, can you? Are you a bloodhound or something? How about I bury it, and you try to find it like a dog too!"

He was trying to be funny. He took out the cash and held it up. Violet furiously reached for it. She couldn't get it. He held it too high for her, and his friends laughed at her efforts.

Despite being unable to reach the money, Violet kept trying. It was almost as if she had to prove herself in that situation and not back down.

After spending a good chunk of time struggling for the money, Violet looked at the ground in frustration, her blood boiling, and cursed at the boy as loud as she could, "Drop dead!"

Immediately, the boy's face went blank, dropping to the ground within seconds.

Oh no! The magic ring!

The ring had taken what she said as a wish and killed him instantly. Realizing what had happened, she forgot about the money and ran.

She ran out of the school and made a bee-line for the forest behind the building.

I'm sorry! I am so SORRY!

Violet never wanted to hurt anyone; she did not mean for this to happen. All she could think about was how her parents would react knowing that their daughter killed a child and how that child's parents would feel knowing that their son was dead.

All Violet could think at that point was how she should have let him have the money. It was only four dollars, and she could have gotten four more from her dad the next day. Or wished for a million she had the magic ring!

She could have had anything she wanted; why take someone's life for just 4 dollars? Millions of thoughts ran through Violet's mind as she made her way to the forest, panicked and scared for her life.

Terrified of what had just happened and even more scared of what would happen going forward. She did not care that she would miss the rest of that day's classes. She had just killed a kid. That kid's face was all that she could think of.

It was almost as if the kid's face was playing on repeat and looping in her head.

Hopefully, people did not make the connection between her and the kid. She hoped they thought it was a stroke or something. Violet's mind was not rationalizing anything; she could not make sense of anything.

All her innocent mind could comprehend at that time was that she had just killed a kid who did not deserve to die like that.

After a while, she stopped in a clearing, her mind racing.

She sat down on a large rock but wished she was back home. Walking back home, she missed the ambulance that came to pick up the dead boy and the threats that would have come from his friends.

Afraid she would go to the juvie, she walked into her house, looking for her parents and the support that they could provide. Her parents weren't there.

Violet started to panic. What would she do? She could not spend the rest of her life in prison!

That is when it occurred to her that the best thing to do in such a dire situation is to leave and never return, and that is precisely what she did.

She wanted to leave a note so her parents wouldn't worry. She was not quite sure when to do it. No doubt his friends would vengefully tell the police what happened and maybe even say she meant to do it.

Wondering if the ring was evidence, she took it off and put it in her pocket. At that moment, nothing Violet did would have made sense, and nothing she would do make sense, either. At that time, all she could think about was what would happen. How far could this go?

Violet didn't have much to take and stuffed all her belongings in a pillowcase. She had some savings from last year that she had kept for some shoes, so she took these too. Then she wrote her parents a note and told them not to worry. Only Violet knew how there was so much to worry about, especially when the police were after her. Violet took her father's sleeping bag. There was enough money from her savings to get her to Canada by train. She hurriedly headed for the train station, bought a ticket, and boarded.

In her mind, Violet was fully aware that this was not something she had planned; however, she was still running away, and that too to Canada... an uncharted territory for her.

The train ride was a long one. There were many things for Violet to go through in her head; she had to clear her mind of everything that had happened.

But how could she? In her mind, Violet was still guilty of murdering someone; that was the only thing she could think of and what would happen to her and her family.

Violet was terrified that despite having a ring that could take her anywhere, she did not think of using it.

Instead, she boarded a train headed to Canada. Not knowing the ring's power, Violet could have just asked for this memory to become distant and be forgotten by everyone, but she still chose to run away.

It had been three days and two nights since it happened. In other words, the world would have changed. But not for Violet; for her, it was still shocking. Time had slowed down for her, and she was in the center of it all.

She did not want to go to her grandmother's, but it was the only place she could go. Her grandma was widowed and lived near the Canadian border that connects to America.

She would arrive there on her birthday. This was not how Violet planned her birthday, and that is not how her family planned it, either.

Things just changed so fast that she could not even say goodbye as she wanted. The thought of a goodbye never really occurred to her, to begin with.

Maybe there was even something she could help with around the house. There was so much time on her hands now that she was away from a troublesome place where her life was in danger but was Violet's life really in danger, or was she just being paranoid about the whole situation? Her grandmother was old and lived alone.

When Violet checked her email, she saw that grandma had wished her pre-emptively for her birthday. That was her opportunity to tell her she was coming and let her know she did not want her mother to know where she was.

And so, she decided to make a call.

***

To Violet's surprise, her grandma was understanding and offered to come to get her. She could stay with her in rural Canada. Away from it all. Away from all the horrors that presumably waited for her back in America, a place where the authorities were out to get her and incarcerate her.

For Violet, there were different and peaceful places, unlike America's chaotic, busy life. She started liking it, or maybe it was the feeling she would get after being away from a seemingly hostile place.

Violet thought this could be a new start for her, and she could hopefully continue her education there. She did not want to stay at home all the time and throw away her life like that.

It was too expensive to get a private room, but still, the seat next to the window was good, and she enjoyed it a lot more than one would think.

"Is this seat taken?" a young man asked her.

She saw he was tan with shiny brown hair and a nice white button-down shirt. His brown eyes were amber. He looked about nineteen or twenty.

As if she had forgotten his question, she answered, "No, of course not. Go ahead."

He was the most attractive young man she had seen. It momentarily broke her out of her reveries and allowed her to think in the present and think where she was at the moment.

"My name's Curtis. It looks like we're going the same way."

"I'm going to my grandmother's house. I can't wait. My birthday is in a few days."

"Great," Curtis answered, and they talked together into the afternoon, glad to be sitting next to one another. They talked about everything that one could talk about.

In those moments, Violet felt normal once again, as if everything that happened before was just a nightmare that had come to an end, and this was a fresh start for her.

"Have you been on a train before?"

"No." Violet looked at the ground to stop staring at him. She was struggling, and although Violet found Curtis very attractive, it was a good way of keeping her mind off everything that had happened earlier that week.

"I have. It's pretty comfortable. I'm glad I got to leave. I couldn't wait to get out of the city."

"My grandma lives near some farms. She is coming to get me there."

"Stick with me. We can get a blanket from the train staff for the night."

They stared out the window as they drove through the valley. Curtis talked more about himself, and Violet was happy to listen. He was from Anaheim.

Violet, on the other hand, was glad that she started to get to know more and more about Curtis; it finally felt like she had a human connection, something that had become

rare.

He picked up a book and began reading. Violet looked out the window. They sat together in peace.

"You would think they would have magazines here," Violet said as they headed through Northern California.

She smiled and tried not to look stupid because she had a crush on him.

"I'm going to call my grandma." She did want to. She just also wanted to brush her hair and apply a little makeup.

She stood up.

"Oh, what's her name?"

"Abigail"

She stood up and headed towards the other car. It was evening, and she felt nervous that her parents would know she hadn't come home. She decided to call her grandma again.

Her grandmother did say when she arrived, she would call her mother and let her know where she was. Violet frowned, but her nerves went away.

"I guess that's best. What about school?"

"We will have to get you in here."

"I wrote a note, but my mom will call the police."

"I'll call her tonight and stop her. She doesn't trust anyone more than her mom. I can't wait for you to come, dear! We can go to church, shop, and work on the farm. I'll see you soon," she said in her kind old lady voice.

"I'll see you," Violet said as she sat staring at the bathroom.

"Sounds good."

***

Violet and Curtis spent the next hour getting to know each other and ate dinner. They chatted about fun stuff and the books he was into that night. Then darkness fell.

Violet had a feeling that it was going to be all right. After a long, long time, she finally had a glimmer of hope that when all of this passed away, things would get better for her and all of it would be over soon.

"They will have dinner in less than an hour," he said when she returned.

After dinner, they received blankets, watched the night sky, and talked.

"I'm going to Canada to see my dad," he said.

"I am going to live there. I've only been there once when I was little."

"Do you want to go out with me?'

"And be your girlfriend?" she asked excitedly.

"Yes. I mean, I like you. We can get to know the place together. There are endless possibilities for us."

"I would love to." They both smiled and agreed. The sky was full of stars as they entered the Oregon border. "I wonder what my mom is doing. If she's pissed that I'm over here. Can I be honest with you?"

"Yes."

"I ran away. That's why I think my parents would be mad. My dad let me, a teenager, keep a magic ring. It's their fault, honestly. I had it on and wished for some bully to die, and he did! I didn't know he would. It was not really like I wanted it to happen for real."

Instead of being freaked out when she started talking about a magic ring or thinking she was crazy, Curtis just seemed to roll with it. At that moment, he did not care much about her actions.

Violet was too distressed to pay the absurdity of the situation any mind. She was glad he did not laugh at her or call her crazy. It seemed he was concerned, as any other ordinary and sensible person would be. That was all Violet needed at that moment, a moment of normalcy.

"That sounds serious. Does anyone know?"

"No, no one but his friends. I first wished I got home, but then it did something bad. I don't know what it is capable of."

"You'll be safe in Canada."

Violet nodded in agreement and closed her eyes. She kept thinking about how she just wanted things to pass now and to go back to normal.

She knew that this would not be easy, but at the same time, she was trying her best to tell herself that everything that had happened was not her fault. She would not have known the extent of that ring's power.

Chapter 4:
The Train

In the morning, when she woke up, the train was going through the Washington mountains. On her way to the bathroom, she noticed a newspaper.

She read the headline in absolute horror:

Misty Falls, CA Sam Cardinal falls dead at high school. Funeral this weekend. Parents and community members were devastated by the shocking death.

And there was the picture of the boy she killed, the same boy who had stolen her money. At that moment, the memories of the incident started playing in her head all over again, it was as if something had set Violet off, and she knew that everyone was about to find out who killed Sam.

She grabbed the paper and dropped it in front of Curtis.

She wanted him to know about what had happened.

"This is the guy I killed."

He lifted the paper, reading what she showed him. His eyes went wide in shock

"Oh my gosh, it is true! The guy is dead. That's going to come back to you. I thought you were kidding or something. They're going to come after you now."

He cringed when she went white at what he had said. He hugged her and tried to comfort her. Curtis realized that his words were not kind to someone freaking out and in dire need of comfort.

"Hey, I'm your boyfriend. I'll protect you." He held her hand and kissed it.

Upset, Violet dropped to her seat. Curtis didn't want to say anything. It had killed the mood for her last day on the train. The past few days felt like Violet was out of all the trouble and terrible things that happened to her, and here she was again, back in the same rut from which she escaped.

Violet tried to recover a little, focusing on what was ahead. Canada, her grandmother, Curtis, and a new life that was waiting for her. New school, new people to meet, and so many new opportunities. She could have a whole new life full of options, and no one would ever bother her.

However, at that moment, it was hard for her to focus on what was happening around her. In the back of her mind, she had still killed Sam, and she kept thinking about how, sooner or later, people would find out about what had happened and who was responsible for it.

Once the authorities figure out who killed Sam, it will be over for Violet; this little dream with Curtis, her time with Darkness, and her family, everyone will suffer because of the mistake made on Violet's part.

She tried not to worry about what the future held for her. She turned to Curtis,

"I'm sorry. We'll go out. You will come over on my birthday, and we'll watch a scary movie together. My grandma's house is big enough. It's out in the country. It will be just the three of us. We'll be safe there."

Curtis nodded in agreement smiling at her. He was glad she tried to look to the future and not dwell on what had happened. Guilt is something a person cannot carry through their life, and even though one would not call Violet guilty, in her mind, things were different.

"In the meantime, I wish I'd brought something to read. Something to take my mind off things." She took the newspaper.

"Who are you going to stay within Canada?"

"My uncle. He owns a dairy farm; my dad wants me to work on it and attend school. I got into trouble for ditching school, not doing homework, and not listening to my parents."

"We'll be better together. I have a good feeling about this.

We'll have our first day of school together. Are you sixteen?"

"Yeah, sixteen and a half."

"That's why you're so tall."

They both laughed a little. She felt a little better.

"I'm going to call my grandmother and grab breakfast."

"Okay, I'll call home too."

She hugged him, and they were off to do what they had to. Once again, Violet had started looking forward to the prospect and how this could finally be it.

The day on the train was a little boring until they learned they would stop on the Washington coast for a few hours.

"The beach!"

It appeared to her to be incredibly beautiful. Large starfish tan and coral colored could be seen from the train, only ten minutes from the station.

The beach would do wonders for her spirits after the gloomy day.

***

"Don't tell anyone," she told Curtis and pulled a wad of cash, twenties, from her backpack. They were walking on the sand together as they talked.

"I took it from my parents. I had some savings, but I grabbed some from my dad's drawer. I had to. That's why I can't go back home soon. They would kill me."

She was still anxious, despite the calming effects of the rolling tide. Although she was trying her best to live in the present, a part of her mind was constantly in the past, as if something from her past was pushing her back.

"That's way more than I got." He pulled a few dollars from his pocket. "I'll buy us lunch."

It was a deal, and they spent lunchtime on the beach eating. They had a nice little picnic to take their minds off things.

Finally, something good was happening in her life once again as she had Curtis keep her company and reassure her that he would not abandon her despite everything that had happened and would happen.

After having pizza Violet collected as many shells as she could and stuck them in her backpack zipper pocket. Then she sat by him under a tree in the shade. This was a muchneeded relaxation for her that would have allowed her to take her mind off things.

The spring sun was beating down, contrasting the cool sea breeze. It was delightful on the beach. It was obvious that Violet and Curtis were enjoying their time on the beach; things looked normal; they could both have fun and not worry about what was to come.

"I can't wait for summer. We'll go to the beach. Ever been surfing?"

"A couple of times. Not my thing."

"I'll get you into it. We'll have to exchange numbers in case we get separated." She wrote down hers, and he did the same.

"We should be getting back."

The engine started up as they boarded just in time to not be left behind.

***

It was easy to take a nap with the sound of the train to provide ambient noise. After all, their time at the beach relaxed enough for them to rest and look toward the future.

When she woke, it was early evening. Curtis said, "Dinner will be ready soon."

She couldn't wait to see her grandma in the morning. She picked up her newspaper to do crossword puzzles until dinner came. She was distracted by the mystery until the thoughts came racing back into her mind, making her anxious.

She could not help but think about everything that happened and how everything would change her life. The thoughts were racing back and forth, and even the puzzle was not enough to calm her down.

"Everyone saw."

"Huh?" He looked concerned.

"When Sam Cardinal dropped dead, everyone saw him, and my friend was there. I need to call my mother."

She left him there, changing her mind about cutting off all contact with her parents. She could not do it anymore. How can one just get up and leave everything behind? Trying to tell themselves that whatever happened is okay and things will return to normal again.

Their dinner arrived, and he had them leave some for her as he waited for her to return.

When she returned, she said, "I tried to explain why I was going to grandma. They are suspicious, but no one knows about the ring killing him. Can you keep it a secret?" "Of course."

"I had to tell her I would pay her back and not get into trouble with the ring. The cops aren't after me after all! What in the world do they think that guy's cause of death is?"

"I don't know, but that ring is protecting you."

"What should I wish for now?"

"That we could eat. I'm starving."

"I'll wish for dessert."

An announcement over the train speaker called out, "Stay in your seats. Dessert will be served shortly. We will arrive at our destination at nine a.m."

Minutes later, they had slices of chocolate cake with Violet happy, and Curtis worried about what that ring could do. For Violet, the cake at that moment was everything, but Curtis could not help but wonder what other powers the ring possessed and whether it could harm him.

It was their last night on the train, and the dark mountains looked foreboding, a wolf ran through the trees, but the stars shone in the moonless night. Both of them marveled at the beauty of the milky way.

While Curtis slept, Violet snuck a kiss on his cheek. She felt sleepy as she thought about her next wish. To take back some of the mistakes she had made, but staring into the night, she assumed there was no taking back Sam Cardinal's death.

She wasn't sure she wanted to, but he was so young, and the death was a tragedy. She was plagued with terrible dreams about Sam, Canada, and the ring when she fell asleep. Its power shone like a ray that would affect everything it touched. She woke afraid and leaned against a sleeping Curtis.

The noise of talking woke Curtis early, so he woke Violet up. Shortly the announcements came that soon they would stop at their destination, and they were in Canada. They could see nothing but land. It didn't seem the way she remembered it, but she hadn't been there since she was eleven. Again, a wave of peace passed through her as she thought about how this could change everything for her.

As soon as the train pulled up, she saw her grandmother waiting for her.

"Let's go," she said to him. She grabbed her backpack and duffle bag, and his clothes.

They stepped off the train, hand in hand, to explore the new horizons waiting for them, away from all the turmoil that stood for Violet back in America.

Chapter 5:
Canada! Oh, Canada!

"Grandma, this is Curtis, my boyfriend."

Upon leaving the station, Violet could spot her grandmother waiting to greet her. They had just met, and she wanted her to know about Curtis immediately.

"Hi, kids!" she nodded at them, giving them both a meaningful look. Violet could see how excited her grandmother was to see her and how she was looking forward to knowing more about her.

"You just met?" Grandma's long grey hair was in a bun, and she wore a dark blue dress with a sweater. Her entire personality was warm and welcoming, exactly what Violet needed in such dire times.

"Yes, he was coming my way," she responded. "He was going to come over for my birthday."

"Alright. Say goodbye, and I'll call your mother."

They both stepped away to say their goodbyes and hugged. The hug was what Violet needed the most at that time; it was almost like a reassurance that told her everything would be okay.

"Wait, how are you going to get to my house?"

"A horse." They both laughed. "I don't know. Maybe I can get a ride later. I'll see you. My uncle's here."

"Bye."

It turned out they lived only fifteen minutes apart from each other; this meant that meeting each other would be a lot easier for them.

The house and area were as she remembered it from having visited a long time ago. The house was brown with hundreds of pine trees and a beautiful lake that was good for swimming in the summertime. Her grandma lived alone, and Violet got her room.

"Is that the ring you were telling me about?" her grandma asked.

"Yes. My dad says it has magical powers. There's a long story involved. My dad told me about it."

Violet blamed her father for telling her that so her grandmother would not laugh at the idea of magic. It was as if she was trying to shift the blame to her father for telling her about the ring in the first place.

"Well," she started with a chuckle, "I hope it's magic enough to help me around the house. Anyways, when do I start school?"

"Next Monday, when I have you signed up. They will have your classes."

"I think Curtis and I will go to the same school."

"We'll have pizza for dinner tonight, and I made you a vanilla cake. I also borrowed a little boat from a gardener who works here so you can have it for the little lake. Happy birthday, my Vi." She smiled a sweet smile.

Violet's face lit up. She loved being in nature; she loved being in Canada with her grandmother. Everything felt normal at that moment. As if everything is going to get better for her, she could finally have an everyday life in Canada.

"Oh, good. I think I'm going to love it here. How long can I stay?"

"As long as your mom allows it, it looks like you'll be here at least the school year."

"Grandma, you know I'm used to country living, being from Misty Falls. It's beautiful there. I'm so excited! This ring is going to bring me whatever I want."

"What?" she asked, puzzled, pulling into the dirt driveway.

"Nothing, I'm just saying this is a lucky magic ring. I wish it did homework, too," Violet said sarcastically.

While they were talking, a light brown chubby corgi came from around the corner to see them.

"Oh, he's cute."

"That's Muffin," grandma Abigail said.

The dog followed them into the house, and Violet went straight to her old room. Muffin followed her in, and she sat by it.

"You're as chubby as a muffin, aren't you?" she asked, petting it.

The dog looked happy to have made a new friend. The room looked the same: brown carpet, yellow walls, and tan furniture. There was one window on the left side of the room, which was enormous. The sun was beating down, and she opened the window to let some in.

It was the second story; the room looked over the area, and the lake was visible. There were two swans near the water. Violet took a picture with her phone and sent it to her mom, saying, *Don't worry; I'll be all right. Everything's peachy here.*

Her mom responded*, That's good, Vi, and do your homework, but someone broke in this afternoon. We came home to find a window broken and the house a mess—especially your room. I only noticed they stole your jewelry box, but it only had fake jewelry. Did you take that ring you found?*

Yes, I have it, thank God.

Good, we've called the police. I'll talk to you every day. Do your homework when school starts. We miss you.

How could this be related to what happened to Sam? Was someone after her? So, she texted her mom one last time to learn more about the situation and to be certain that everything was good and new and that nothing was going wrong for her or her family.

Mom, don't tell anyone where I am. I start school Monday, and I met a boy on the train. His name's Curtis, and he's going to go to my school.

Her mother agreed not to tell anyone. Because of the events that had happened the last few days, Violet was tired and hungry and badly needed a shower. Although she was tired, she had this fleeting sense that things would be fine for her once more as she headed to school and things started getting better.

She put off calling Curtis because he may not even be home yet and hopped into the shower, which was to be followed by lunch and a nap in a nice warm bed. Her grandma had left a nice warm blanket for her. She turned on the shower, and her stomach growled unhappily.

Lucky for her, her grandma had already gotten pizza when she was done showering.

"How did you know I was so hungry?" she asked with a skip.

"Easy guess. The cake you will have tonight," her grandma gently said.

"Okay. Can I call Curtis to come over for some?'

"Sure. It's your sweet sixteen. We should have a big party."

"No, that's okay. I just got here. My boyfriend and I are fine." She stepped away to call him.

"He said he would come after they go to the feed and seed. He has to work on the farm because he got into trouble at home." She squinted her eyes at her grandma. "How well do you know this boy?"

"I just met him on the train." she said while she played with her ring. She wanted to tell her grandma about wishing for a birthday present.

She grabbed some pizza and went upstairs. She shut the door and sat on the floor, wanting to wish for Curtis. Knowing that would anger him, she tried to think of something else. Her mom had sent her a text saying they sent her a package for her birthday, but it would be getting there late.

The phone text was the perfect form of communication for her mother to keep after her. It sounded good. The doorbell rang; it was Curtis.

"Hi," he said.

"Hi, I have pizza."

He entered and grabbed some pizza.

Violet followed. "Let's go up to my room. I'll show you a view of the lake. My grandma borrowed a boat we can take on it."

They headed to the room and looked out over the area through the window. There were scratches at the door, and Muffin entered. They ran down the stairs to the front door, and Muffin followed. Curtis opened the door.

"No, Muffin, you stay there," she said, and they walked towards the lake.

There was a big silver rowboat, and they pushed it by the lake. Mountains were nearby, and a cool spring breeze blew. The farms were more east.

"I live that way," he pointed down the road going right. It was the perfect afternoon. They pushed the boat into the water and got in. It floated towards the middle. Violet giggled. She had never been on a ship before. Far behind them, they heard a fish jump. They laid down; everything was relaxing ... peaceful. Just what a 16-year-old could want on her birthday.

"I love Canada."

"I like it too," he agreed.

"I like you." Violet kissed him. Wind blew. It was all meant to be. It all felt right, like the perfect puzzle completing itself. Everything felt as if it was supposed to happen. Maybe it was all planned. Perhaps that is precisely what fate wanted in the first place.

"I start school Monday."

"So do I. I'll meet you by the admin office that morning. I'll bet we'll have some of the same classes."

"Mhmm," was all that came back at that time. Violet was too lost in the moment; she did not want to think of anything else.

"Violet, happy birthday," he said.

"Thanks. I heard from my mom the guys that broke into their house were Sam Cardinal's friends. They found out I was the last person talking to him. I don't know how, but I think they know about the ring. They stole my jewelry box. There wasn't much in it. It doesn't matter now; they'll be caught and imprisoned before long."

"It may not matter. They could get out and be angry."

"I'm here. With this ring, I have luck."

"What if that luck changes?"

"It won't. I just need to figure out what to wish for next."

"How about a giant beanstalk." They laughed, and he kissed her on the head.

"I wish. What would I do with one? How about you receive a car? We can go very far."

"Try it," he said, and his breath quivered.

"I wish Curtis had a car for us. Any car." A big sparkle came out of the ring.

Mainly because it was sunny, but maybe it was working its magic. Violet did not know at the moment, and she was not sure about what had happened at that moment, but it did not matter. Violet knew about the ring's power, so she was confident something would come out of it, too.

Whatever the case, Violet was happy to be with her boyfriend. Everything at that moment was perfect. A thought crossed her mind that maybe everything that had happened previously was leading up to this situation, and her being in Canada and with Curtis was bound to happen in the first place.

She quickly phased out all the thoughts away from her mind and tried to focus on the moment she spent with Curtis.

Chapter 6:
Grandmother's House

The next day as Violet sat on her bed watching TV and petting Muffin, there was a loud honk outside. She ran out the front door, and there it was.

Outside her house was an old convertible, rusting and ready to fall apart; the car looked like it barely survived the test of time.

The door had opened, and Curtis had stepped out.

"I got home, and there it was, waiting for me. My uncle said he got it for me so I would have something to drive to school. I can pick you up Monday."

She wasn't sure she wanted to be seen in that car.

Frowning, she said, "Okay, good."

She was in love with him and would do this for him. It did not matter that the car was a rust bucket.

He came and hugged her. "Let's go."

She ran and grabbed her phone, and they were gone.

Monday morning, as Violet left the office with her list of classes, she ran into Curtis.

"I didn't see you. Let me see your classes." He held the list to her eyes.

"We have two classes together." She hugged him.

"Sit as close to me as you can. Now let's find our lockers."

They walked in that direction. Their lockers were close by too. They waved goodbye and were off to their first class of the day. Things looked good for them; Curtis now had a car, was in the same school, and shared classes. It all felt like a perfect plan falling into place.

***

The rest of the day went well. In the last period of study hall together, Violet hadn't spoken much to him, so she wrote him a note. They didn't get caught; they were quiet because no one knew each other yet.

After class, they went to a nearby deli.

Violet's ring was on her hand, and the six large diamonds sparkled in the light. They sat at a table and ordered subs. The door was jerked open, and someone came in. He had slick black hair and a black jacket.

"Give me that ring," he roared. "And that cash."

One of the employees heard it and called the cops. The employee was in the back, and the mugger didn't know he was there.

Not wanting to part with the ring, she ignored him, and a female employee distracted him by opening the cash register drawer and giving it all to him.

When Violet turned around, he had a gun on her.

He pointed the gun back at her and screamed at her, "Lay on the ground."

She did as he wished and then whispered to her ring, "Help get rid of him. I can't part with you."

It did as she wished. His gun fired. The bullet ricocheted off some metal dishes and hit him in the forehead, killing him on the spot. However, unlike the incident with Sam,

Violet wanted the mugger dead; he was not just a threat to Violet and her ring but to Curtis, everyone in the shop, and, ultimately, the city.

Violet did nothing after his death; she did not want to touch the body. All she did was wait for the police to arrive, and once they did, she told everyone that he had shot himself by accident.

The cops inquired about the incident, asked her to tell them everything, took her name, and then told her that she was free to leave.

The deli incident was not the first time the ring had defended itself from being taken away from her. It was becoming more and more evident that the ring was not just powerful in granting wishes, but it could also defend itself. Violet was not sure if it was a good thing.

When meeting friends at the Great Lakes, they decided they wanted to go swimming. Violet took off her ring, put it on the ground, and swam away.

When the thief came to see it and reached to take the ring, it defended itself with magic. A large wave came in hard and fast. She had swept away to the sea! Violet came in and put the ring on, not realizing what had happened.

The ring was excellent and magical until one afternoon. Violet was chopping celery when the ring started showing signs of hostility.

It wasn't on her finger, but an animal was outside, making a noise. Probably a raccoon was burgling the trashcans outside.

It made her mad, and she exclaimed, "I wish that would stop."

The noise stopped. Violet didn't know until she stepped outside and was shocked to discover what had happened. The power in the ring killed the raccoon in perhaps the most gruesome way, with its bones picked clean.

This moment scared Violet of the ring for the first time. Yes, it had helped her in the past, but now, the ring was showing signs of hostility, and this made Violet think about what would happen if the ring turned on her and the ones she loved.

Soon Violet would lie up at night and leave the ring on the kitchen counter. She would wear it when her hands were in water or cooking.

But two or three nights a week, scary sounds came from the kitchen area. There was scratching and ticks like the house were settling, but it wasn't. It was difficult, and Violet wouldn't go out of fear of what might be waiting for her outside.

One night hearing the sounds, she jumped up, shut and locked her door. Somehow, she fell asleep and heard in her dream a voice calling, "Violet, you're Violet."

In the dream, a purple light had taken her name and called her a murderer because it knew she had killed two people. This moment truly terrified Violet; it almost felt like she was caught, and something terrible was about to happen to her.

Her grandma was asleep and couldn't do anything to help Violet at that point, and she did not want to wake her up, either.

Terrified and uneasy, Violet decided to do some research on the ring. That was when she learned about the monkey's paw. Enchanted objects that granted wishes, but there was always a catch. According to the stories she read, these things always ended badly.

The ring would grant her a wish, but, in the end, it would always take something, if not from her, then around from her. There was no extent to what the ring could take.

She called her mother and let her know she missed her. Her mother was so thrilled! After an hour of research, she was too tired and decided to find the magician. She would get the name from her parents.

At that moment, Violet wanted to ensure that this stopped and the ring caused no more damage. Everything that transpired so far was enough for Violet to be scared

for her life.

The ring had some evil conscience and was more than okay with doing something that was not considered human or even normal to others.

Violet had to get rid of the ring somehow or do something that would mitigate the power of the ring. What if there was a way to stop the ring from hurting other people and still retain its powers?

Violet was terrified, but at the same time, she had to figure out a solution to this problem that just seemed to get out of hand at that point.

Chapter 7:
Lifting The Curse

Come morning, the ring was still on the kitchen counter and not with Violet like it used to be.

Things had become clear that Violet wanted to be away from the ring as much as possible because anything else would make the situation get out of hand, and that was not what anyone wanted.

When grandma Abigail got up, she asked, "Can I keep this ring locked in your safe with your jewelry? There have been two robbing attempts. The diamonds are quite big."

"Yes, of course. Just hand it to me, then I'll run to the store. It's funny, summer is almost here, and I want to knit, but it's too hot. I'll start knitting us sweaters in the fall."

"Thank you, grandma. The ring will be safe, and it won't hear any of my wishes through that steel."

"What?" Abigail looked puzzled. She was unsure what Violet was saying, but she still went ahead and listened to her granddaughter.

"I may pawn that ring." She handed grandma Abigail the ring. She wanted to get rid of it and tried to figure out all the ways she could get rid of that ring. Pawning it... destroying it... throwing it away. There were so many ways.

"Your cousins may come to visit this summer. Ones you've never met. All but one are infants, three and under." She headed to her massive walk-in closet with the sage under some clothes. It was locked away safely. She went out the door to shop, and immediately Violet texted home to ask for the magician's name.

It came back as Brian True. Now, where was he? She had to act fast before the ring struck again! She had to do something to get in touch with the magician and ask him how all of this could be stopped. No matter whether Violet wanted the ring, at that moment, she was no longer okay with the fact that the ring was a dangerous artifact capable of hurting many people.

When she looked him up, he was in Las Vegas. It wasn't very likely she could go there, so she wanted to call. Sadly, she said, "I wish I could win the lottery," to her surprise, nothing happened. It appeared that now the ring was in the safe, it was no longer working, and Violet did not know the combination to the safe either. For a fleeting moment, she was pleased but, at the same time, she was not in a good mood.

Discouraged, she went to buy a lottery ticket with her lunch money. It was quickly forgotten. She scratched her ticket and found she had won two hundred and fifty dollars! And it wasn't the ring this time. Now she had spending money and couldn't wait to tell grandma.

She wanted to spend more time with her grandma. They would go out to dinner, parties, and shop. That night her mother asked, "Where's your ring?"

"I left it at home. I don't want to look at that rotten ring now."

"This came for you." She handed Violet an envelope. It was a letter.

"*Dear Violet, you wrapped me up and locked me away. It wasn't that hard to get out! I am magic, you know. You can use me all you want, but I will continue to harm you. I can't wait for you to come home and find me. Ha ha ha.*"

It was even signed "*Ring.*"

It was dark, and she saw the purple light.

It felt like the floor beneath Violet's feet had disappeared for a second, and her heart had drowned. Moments later, her heart started pounding out of her chest. She woke drenched in sweat. Beginning to think it was just a dream, Violet heard a few clicking noises downstairs coming from her grandma's room.

There was no way she was going down to check it.

Shortly afterward, she fell back asleep.

She still wanted to keep the ring and do good with it.

That night at dinner, she ate lasagna and felt she couldn't wait to check on that ring. And she didn't think her mother would believe her or the police.

So, she anxiously went back to her grandma's room to look for it. When she got to that closet, it wasn't there. She looked in corners and under beds but didn't find it. Violet decided to talk to her grandmother about the ring and find out where it went.

Violet asked her grandmother about the whereabouts of the ring, and her grandmother reassured her, "It's in the closet under the clothes, silly."

They went to the closet, and grandma lifted the clothes pile. She opened the safe, and the ring was in it. "Just let me know if you want it."

That night Violet went to bed thinking happily that the ring may be gone.

***

One night there was a loud crash, and she got up to see what it was. The safe with the ring was in the closet in the middle of the doorway. She missed wearing it and wanted to put it on again. She tip-toed out, planning to ask grandma for it soon.

Curtis was right. It was the monkey's paw. The ring was doing everything on its own, and whatever it would do, it was not good. It was not suitable for Violet or anyone else around her. This was the time for her to decide what she had to do with the ring. She could not just sleep on it or hope that it would stop.

The next day was Sunday, and she wore her ring while it sparkled in the sun. Violet didn't mind that and wanted to see Curtis.

Being away from the ring and Curtis for some time made her realize she wanted to use the ring again. This prompted her to go ahead and make a wish. So another wish was made.

"I want to spend time with Curtis tonight."

There was a big sparkle of light, and the phone rang. It was Curtis. He wanted to watch a scary movie with her at his house that night. Gladly she accepted, happy he didn't know she had wished for it. Now the feral ring just needed to put together the perfect late-night date.

The night was young, and the crickets chirped. Violet had her grandma's permission to have a date night. Curtis had provided for the whole thing. They got some pizza, then popcorn, soda, and brownies after. It was hard for her to pay attention to the movie, and Curtis kept glancing at the ring.

Just then, her finger started to hurt.

The ring felt tight like it was squeezing and irritating her finger. Violet felt something wet. A single drop of blood dripped from her finger, and she grabbed it.

It fell to the floor. She screamed because blood smeared on her finger. Curtis picked it up, and she ran to the front door. She opened it, but the door closed and locked. The knob wouldn't turn.

"I wish the door would open," Curtis said.

Violet opened the door and ran towards his car. Leaning on it, she said, "Do you want to run away to go to Las Vegas and find Brian True?"

"I can't. That's far, and my car probably wouldn't even make it," he said. "Let me take you home." "To the train station," she demanded.

"Okay. That's almost an hour away through the woods.

Don't you want some clothes?" he asked.

"Yes, and I need my money. I won some in the lottery. It came this morning."

"You don't want just to disappear again."

"I won't. I can call."

"You won't have enough."

"Then give me that ring. You can take me to pawn it."

They got in the car and headed to a local pawn shop.

Violet finally decided it was time to get rid of the ring. Things had gone too far, and it was time to bid farewell to the ring. Once and for good. There was no turning back from this.

Violet could finally start feeling like her life could go back to normal. She had experienced this before, but this time around, it was happening. Pawning the ring was going to be her ticket to freedom, a saving grace from the cursed ring,

"I'll give you one thousand for it." He stared at her.

"Okay, deal," she smiled with joy. She would have money, and the ring would be gone. She watched as he counted ten one-hundred-dollar bills to her. She took them and said, "Finders keepers."

"Put that in your pocket," Curtis said. She did. "Now, you don't have to go. You need to go home and finish the school year. Nevada is far. Why do you need Brian True? The ring is gone."

"You're right. I would feel silly calling him. You do it," she smiled, so relieved.

"Okay, I'll do it for you."

He realized he had never told her that he loved her. They still had two years before graduating. They decided to return to his house, and he would call Brian. His side of the conversation was tense. Violet watched him on the dark bedroom floor.

"Vi, it didn't go well. He didn't want to talk. I only learned that Cara is now married to someone else in Mississippi, and he's no longer doing magic. I don't think he knows anything about the ring being cursed. Now let's have brownies." He happily hugged her. "Let's go this June to stay in my uncle's cabin. It's a couple of hours away. It will be fun."

"I'll ask. Do you think we could get married when I turn sixteen?"

"Yes, that sounds great. Violet Tyler, will you -" he stopped, afraid, realizing he didn't have a ring. "Marry me?"

"Yes," she said, smiling. "You don't need to worry about getting me a ring now."

"I agree. Now let me get those brownies."

"I'd better call my grandma."

He brought brownies as she hung up the phone. "When you think about it, that ring is not that far away right now."

"No, but it will be. We'll leave the doors locked until the morning. I hope this rain doesn't curse our marriage," she said.

Thunder sounded, and the phone rang. Curtis answered it, then hung up. "There was no one there, just a sound like something scratching on glass."

"I don't think my grandma will allow me to go off to a cabin with you. I would have to lie to her. And I'm not telling her we're engaged yet either."

"Okay, you think about what you are going to do."

"I want to be with you. I know that much. Where's your uncle?" she asked.

"He'll be home tomorrow. He had a business meeting." The rain was still pouring down hard, but they weren't worried.

The ring was not their problem; there were other things that both Violet and Curtis had to look forward to. An entire life together, the school, and the future was going to be good with Curtis. The ring was gone; there was nothing to worry about. It would not come in the way of everything they wanted.

Chapter 8:
End Of The Ring

The following day, the severe bald pawn shop worker, Terry, counted his money. The ring he had just bought for one thousand was going to be sold for quite a bit more. He put it in the glass case and marked it for twelve hundred.

Terry was happy, even if the margin was not too much, to begin with. He was pleased that the ring was going to make him some profit. Little did he know then that the ring could not have been valued.

"Had a good day," he said smiling, kissing the money with his dark, greedy lips.

The morning was not bright but dark and rainy. An icy draft blew in, making him shiver. The place had gotten colder and damper by that time. It was as if the ring was controlling how things worked. However, Terry did not know what the ring was capable of.

"I wish it were hotter," he said, and immediately the heat kicked in at ninety-nine degrees. He panicked, not knowing why it was so hot. The ring started doing its thing; it was clear that the intentions that the ring had were anything but benign.

The man looked for a way to shut it off but couldn't find one. It was so hot he ran to the door but couldn't get it open. He went to the back and crawled out the window. He fell but managed to run to his car.

Terry put the keys in the ignition and turned it. The enormous explosion hit the little shop, and it caught fire.

No one else was there, and it burned to the ground, the ring wholly covered with debris. A horrible ending, but at least it was gone. Fire trucks soon appeared to put out the fire.

"I don't think they got much business," one chubby firefighter said to an officer drinking coffee. They inspected it and stepped on burnt crunchy wood.

"I'm sure they had insurance," the officer added.

"Let's go," Curtis told Violet.

They entered the car, and he started it. Heading toward Violet's house, they passed where the pawn shop was. It was burnt down to the ground with a fire truck still there.

"You don't think?" Violet asked, terrified of the ring's assumption that all of this could have been done.

"Nah, maybe." He smiled, and they drove to her house, knowing that the ring was no more.

The gray clouds made the sky look peaceful. It felt like leaving behind a past that had been a problem for everyone. A history where nothing good had ever happened.

Violet missed her mother but was glad that the ring had been destroyed. Violet was free of this curse; the ring, although it brought her some joy, it was also followed by a lot of pain that she had to deal with. Violet was happy that all of this was over, and she was finally looking forward to a life that she would spend now that the ring was not a part of it.

Violet reminisced and how things changed after the ring came into her possession. A part of her wished she had never stumbled across the ring, but at the same time, she realized that if it weren't for the ring, she would have never met Curtis, and so much in her life would have just been an afterthought.

She quickly snapped back to reality and looked towards the horizon; a growing wave of peace flowed through her, and for the first time in a long, long time, she felt that things were back to normal. Nothing could stop the progress that she had made and would be making going forward.

About the Author

Martha has studied writing with Writer's Digest and has an associate's degree in Social Behavioral Science. She has also written poems and songs and even studied screen writing and horror. She still practices writing and likes getting writing prompts. Her favorite author is VC Andrews. She loves curling up with her cat and reading those stories.

Did you love *Found In Misty Falls: A Story of Magic*? Then you should read *Beware of a Cursed Forest*[1] by Martha Wickham!

[2]

How long can a magic ring last?Long enough to get Violet through the worst, then send her through it again. When her new husband and his friends go grave robbing, they dig up a legend. They recover a thousand-year-old ring with a curse. When she finds it she uses it to her advantage like the last ring she owned, and her husband confesses to her how he obtained it. The magic flees from the ring after killing the people it sees deserving, but when it attacks her, Violet knows what she must do. It's go back to grandma's, then Misty Falls.When she goes back her curiosity gets the best of her and she goes with a friend to investigate a murder in the haunted forest. Soon the forest is haunting her, and she is met with the killer, who wants more young blood. Though born on Friday the 13th, she believes in herself. Is she able to escape a streak of bad luck?

Read more at https://readmarthawickham.com/.

---

1. https://books2read.com/u/m0JBe7

2. https://books2read.com/u/m0JBe7

About the Author

Martha has studied writing with Writer's Digest and has an associate's degree. She has also written poems and songs and has even studied screen writing and horror at one time. She still practices writing and likes getting writing prompts, and her favorite author is VC Andrews. Listen to her hot new audiobooks at your favorite retailer.

Read more at https://readmarthawickham.com/.